THIS BOOK DONATED BY:

Emma Ugarcovici

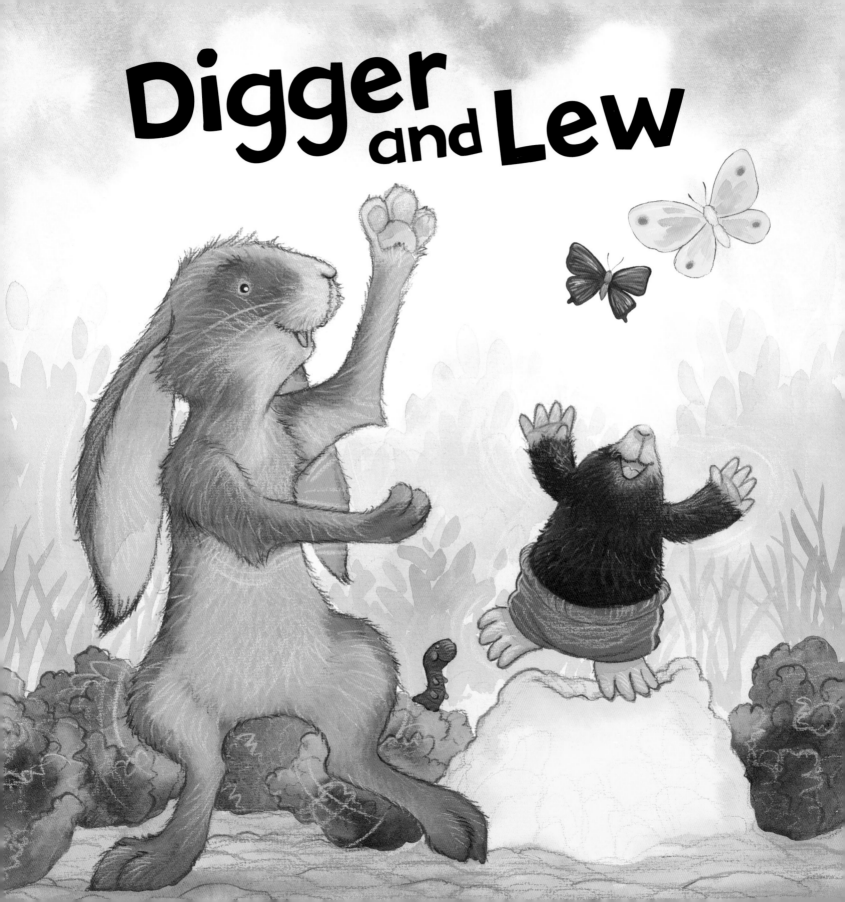

Digger and Lew

Author Malachy Doyle
Illustrator Daniel Howarth
Editor Clare Weaver
Designer Alix Wood
Consultant Anne Faundez

Publisher Steve Evans
Creative Director Zeta Davies

Sandy Creek
122 Fifth Avenue
New York, NY 10011

ISBN 978 1 4351 1659 7

Library of Congress Control Number: 2008011791

Printed and bound in China

10 9 8 7 6 5 4 3 2 1

Digger and Lew

Malachy Doyle
Daniel Howarth

SANDY
CREEK

The sun was bright, the bees were buzzing, and Digger, the mole, popped up from under the ground.

He was right in the middle of the cabbage patch,
and who was there, but Lollopy Lew, the hare.

"What are you doing here, on your fat little legs?"
said Lollopy Lew.
"Have you come to take over my cabbage patch?"

"There's food enough
for both of us,"
squeaked Digger,
blinking at the daylight.
"And my legs are as good
as yours any day."

"Under the ground, they are,"
said Digger, crossly.
"And if you're still here in half
an hour, I'll prove it."

"My darling, my dear, I need your help,"
said Digger to Mrs. Digger,
when he got down to his nest.

"It's time we taught that long-legged hare a lesson."

So they huddled and they muttered...

and they plotted and they planned.

"Are you fit?"
said Digger.

"I'm fit,"
said Lew.

"Are you fast?"
said Digger.

"I'm faster than you!"
said Lew.

"We'll see about that,"
said Digger.
"Now, 1,2,3, go!"

So the hare took off like his tail was on fire, but the mole just popped back under the ground and nibbled a tasty worm.

Yes, Lollopy Lew, he took off like a rocket.
Lollopy Lew, he ran like the wind.

But when he arrived at the
end of the row of cabbages,
up popped a mole.

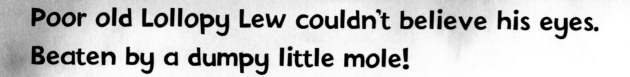

Poor old Lollopy Lew couldn't believe his eyes.
Beaten by a dumpy little mole!

"I'll get you the next time," said Lollopy Lew,
and he turned and dashed back again.

So, Lollopy Lew bounded back to the bottom of the row. But someone was already there...

"You win," said Lollopy Lew, gasping for breath.
"Your legs are as good as mine."

"Are they better?"
said Digger.

So up at one end of the row, there's Digger, digging up his favorite food.

And down at the other end, there's
Mrs. Digger, tucking into hers.

And in the middle,
there's Lollopy Lew,
nibbling cabbage.

And he never guessed that Mrs. Digger
helped Digger to win the race.

Did you?